Splat
and the Big Secret

Based on the bestselling books by Rob Scotton
Cover art by Rick Farley
Text by J. E. Bright
Illustrations by Robert Eberz

HARPER FESTIVAL
An Imprint of HarperCollinsPublishers

HarperFestival is an imprint of HarperCollins Publishers.

Splat the Cat and the Big Secret
Copyright © 2016 by Rob Scotton. All rights reserved.
All rights reserved. Printed in the United States of America.
No part of this book may be used or reproduced in any manner whatsoever without written permission except
in the case of brief quotations embodied in critical articles and reviews. For information address HarperCollins Children's Books,
a division of HarperCollins Publishers, 195 Broadway, New York, NY 10007.
www.harpercollinschildrens.com
Library of Congress Control Number: 2015938891
ISBN 978-0-06-229431-9
Typography by Rick Farley
17 18 19 20   CWM   10 9 8 7 6 5 4 3
❖
First Edition

Splat fitted pieces into a puzzle, hoping his parents didn't notice it was slightly past his bedtime. They were talking in low voices in the kitchen.

Splat's ears perked up when he heard his mother say, "... park next weekend."
"What time does Kitty Kingdom open?" his father asked.

Kitty Kingdom was only the coolest amusement park in the entire universe.

"Is it true?" gasped Splat.
"Is what true?" his mother asked.
"Kitty Kingdom," said Splat. "This weekend. I heard you."

"Yes," his father admitted. "We're all going to Kitty Kingdom on Saturday."
Splat nearly exploded with excitement.
"But don't celebrate yet," warned his father.

"You can't tell anyone," Splat's mother explained. "It's a surprise trip for your sister's birthday. You don't want to ruin her birthday, do you?"
"Promise you won't say anything until Saturday," said his father.

"Can I tell Seymour?" asked Splat.
"No," his father replied. "That mouse can't keep a secret. Can you?"
"I can. I promise," said Splat.

It was lucky that Seymour and Splat's sister were already asleep.
Splat went right to bed himself.
His dreams were all about Kitty Kingdom.

He dreamed he was riding the Panther Commander again and again. Then he took turns on the Whisker and the Lunar Cougar Spaceship!

School on Wednesday seemed so slow. Splat couldn't concentrate. He wanted to yell his secret to everyone in class!

At lunchtime, Spike and Kitten argued about the best ride at Kitty Kingdom. Splat had to stuff his mouth with fish cakes to stop from blurting out his secret.

Splat avoided his sister all evening.
He had to scratch the couch to keep himself from screaming the news.

It had been the longest day of Splat's life.
Seymour was starting to get suspicious that something was up.
Splat couldn't even look him in the eye.

On Thursday, Splat got so riled up that he couldn't sit still after school. He bounced wildly off the walls!

To keep busy on Friday, Splat made paper ducks.
"Are those my birthday present?" his sister asked.
Splat couldn't tell her the real present! He made dozens of nutty-looking ducks instead.

On Friday night, Splat couldn't fall asleep.
He did jumping jacks to wear himself out.
But still he tossed and turned all night.

Splat crawled out of bed early Saturday morning.
"Go ahead, Splat," his mother said, "tell your sister the big news."

Splat erupted with information. "It's so crazy I couldn't tell you the best thing ever but I didn't ruin the secret we're going to Kitty Kingdom today for your birthday I can't believe it's finally here happy birthday I'm so excited I can't even stand it!"

When he saw his sister's look of joy, Splat felt glad he'd kept the secret.

During the long drive to Kitty Kingdom, Splat was exhausted. He nodded off in the car.

Splat's father gently shook his shoulder. "We're here," he said. "C'mon, wake up." They were in the Kitty Kingdom parking lot. Splat still felt so sleepy he couldn't see straight.

Seymour and Splat's sister and father hurried ahead.
Splat's mother helped him stumble toward the entrance. "I expected you to be more excited," she said.
"I've never been happier in my whole life," said Splat.